We Are Shining

Written by **Gwendolyn Brooks**

Illustrated by **Jan Spivey Gilchrist**

HARPER

An Imprint of HarperCollinsPublishers

Acknowledgments

Thank you to each of the puzzle pieces who made this book possible: Jan, Alyson Day
and the rest of the hardworking HarperCollins crew, and of course, Mama.
—Nora Brooks Blakely

Thank you to Mya Michelle Looney, HarperCollins art angels,
Walter Stoller, MD, Regis Lebron, and Kelvin K. Gilchrist, PhD.
—Jan Spivey Gilchrist

HarperCollins
PUBLISHERS
Since 1817

Text originally published as "A Little Girl's Poem" in *Very Young Poets*,
Brooks Press, Chicago, IL. Copyright © 1983 by Gwendolyn Brooks Blakely.
Reprinted with the permission of the Gwendolyn Brooks Estate.

Library of Congress Control Number: 2016949968
ISBN 978-0-06-257066-6

The artist used watercolor to create the illustrations for this book.
17 18 19 20 21   PC   10 9 8 7 6 5 4 3 2 1
❖
First Edition

For Mama, whose words continue
to sing and to shine
—Nora Brooks Blakely

For Women That Soar, Dallas,
and especially for Nora Brooks Blakely
—Jan Spivey Gilchrist

is for **me**
and is **shining!**

and sun and bells and singing.

There are children in the world

all around me and beyond me—

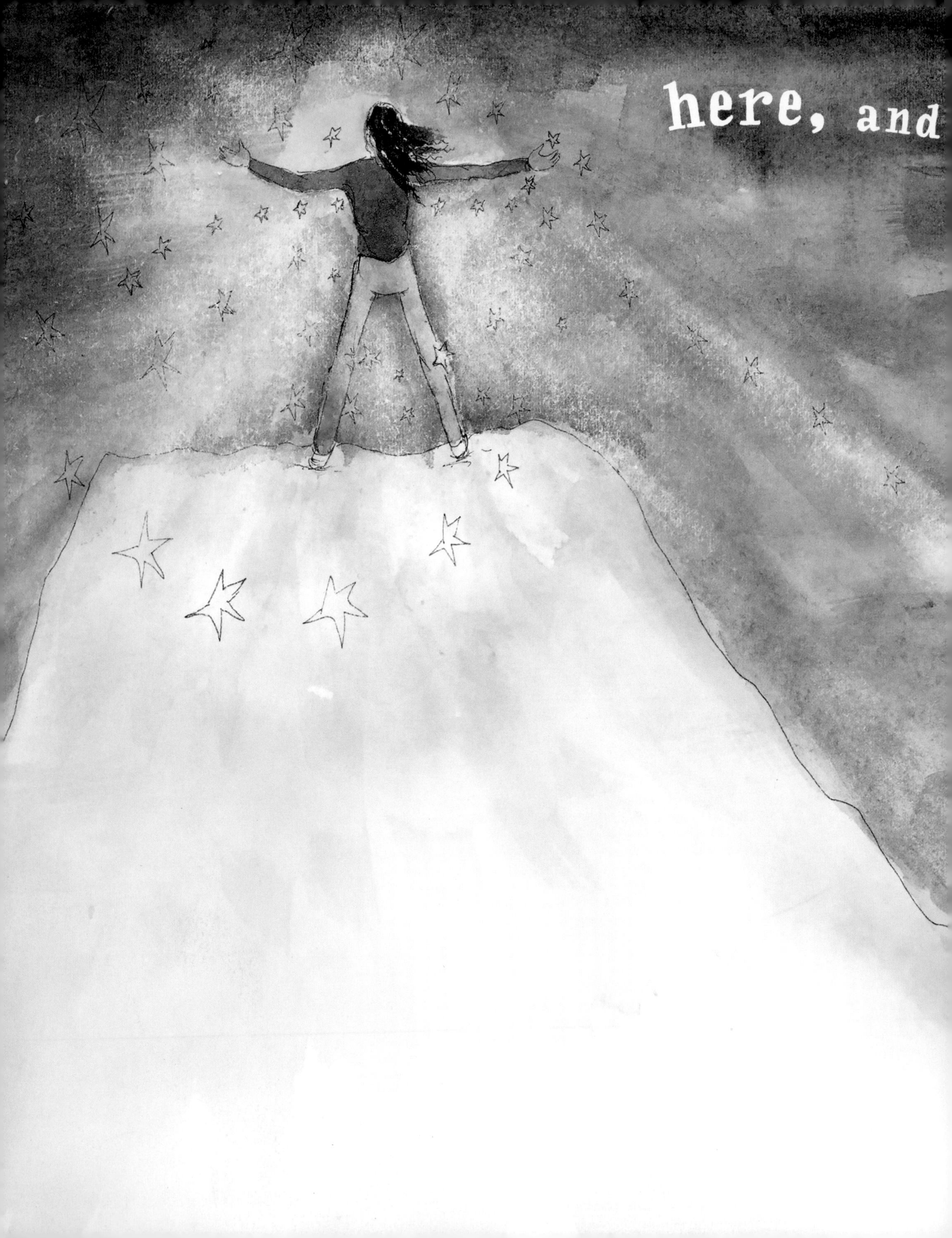

here, and

beyond the big waters;

here,

and in countries peculiar to me

but not peculiar to themselves.

I want the children to live and to laugh.

I want them to sit with their mothers and fathers

and have **happy** cocoa **together.**

I do not want
fire screaming
up to the sky.

I do not want
families killed
in their doorways.

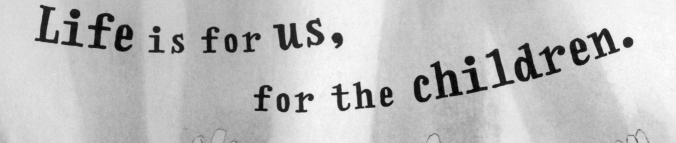

Life is for **us**,
for the **children**.

Life is for
mothers

and **fathers,**

life is for the tall girls and boys in the high school on

Henderson Street,

is for the
people in Afrikan tents,

the people in
English cathedrals,

the **people** in Indian courtyards,

the **people** in cottages all over the world.